Save the School!

Based on the episode "Owlette of a Kind"

Simon Spotlight

New York London Toronto Sydney New Delhi

SIMON SPOTLIGHT

An imprint of Simon & Schuster Children's Publishing Division
1230 Avenue of the Americas, New York, New York 10020
This Simon Spotlight paperback edition July 2019
This book is based on the TV series PJ MASKS © FrogBox/Entertainment One UK Limited/Walt Disney EMEA Productions Limited 2014;
Les Pyjamasques by Romuald © (2007) Gallimard Jeunesse. All Rights Reserved. This book/publication © Entertainment One UK Limited 2019.
Adapted by Lisa Lauria from the series PJ Masks
For information about special discounts for bulk purchases, please contact Simon & Schuster Special Sales at 1-866-506-1949 or business@simonandschuster.com.
Manufactured in the United States of America 0519 LAK
10 9 8 7 6 5 4 3 2 1
ISBN 978-1-5344-3981-8
ISBN 978-1-5344-3982-5 (eBook)

It's a sunny day on the school playground. Amaya, Connor, and Greg are practicing their gymnastics moves.

"I just learned the coolest gymnastics move," Amaya says to Greg and Connor. "It's a forward roll." She lifts her arms in the air. "Want to see?"

Before Amaya can show them, Connor does a perfect forward roll!

"Whoa, that's awesome!" Greg says. "Can you teach me?"

"But . . . the forward roll was supposed to be my thing!" Amaya says.

Suddenly the teacher tells them that the playground shed is completely empty. All the gym mats, paintbrushes, and balls are . . . missing!

Connor, Greg, and Amaya run to the shed. Sure enough everything *is* gone!

"This looks like a job for us," Amaya says.

"PJ Masks, we're on our way!" Connor exclaims. "Into the night to save the day!"

Catboy, Gekko, and Owlette zoom over to HQ and activate the Picture Player. Owlette spots Romeo at the school! "To the Cat-Car!" Catboy says. They race to school.

Inside the school building, the PJ Masks find a trail of the missing items.

Meanwhile Romeo is hiding in one of the classrooms. "Once the PJ Masks trigger my trap, the world will be mine!" he says.

Soon the PJ Masks walk into the classroom.

"Oh, hello," Romeo teases. "I didn't see you there. Were you looking for me?"

"You know we were," Gekko replies.

The PJ Masks are confused. Why would Romeo want to steal gym equipment and paintbrushes? He must have some sort of plan. But what is it?

Owlette flies toward Romeo to find out. At that moment Romeo pushes a button on his device and traps her in a swirling beam!

"What's going on?" Owlette cries. "Put me down!"

"Taking all that stuff was just a way to get you here," Romeo cackles. "Now for my real plan."

Zap! A bright light flashes, and suddenly Romeo is floating in the air!

"I'm flying! With my Power Copier, I've copied your powers," he tells Owlette.

"What?" Owlette shrieks. "No one uses my powers but me!"

Gekko and Catboy fly toward Romeo. It turns out they have Owlette's powers now too. But since they don't know how to fly very well, Romeo manages to escape!

"I'll be seeing you later, Catboy and Gekko, for copies of your powers!" Romeo says as he flies away.

Owlette is annoyed. "Flying is *my* power," she says. "I know how to use it and would've caught Romeo if you two didn't get in the way. Just use your own powers."

"But with double powers, we'll be able to stop him in half the time," Catboy tells her.

"Yeah," Gekko agrees. "Plus, flying is so fun. We've never been able to do this before!"

Just then the PJ Masks hear Romeo calling out to them.
"PJ Masks, come out to play!" Romeo shouts. "These owl powers
are pretty good. But once I get the rest of your powers, I'll be
unstoppable!"

"Come here, little birdies," Romeo giggles. As the PJ Masks zoom towards him, Owlette realizes they are in trouble. "Oh no, it's a trap!" she cries. "Stop!"

But Gekko and Catboy don't know how to stop flying! They head right toward Romeo, who zaps them with his Power Copier.

"Super Cat Speed! Gekko Camouflage!" Romeo cries. He has stolen Catboy and Gekko's powers too!

"Now that I've copied all your powers, nothing can stop me from taking over the world," Romeo laughs.

"This is all my fault," Owlette says sadly. "If I hadn't been so upset about sharing my flying powers, we would have already stopped Romeo."

"That's okay, Owlette," Catboy says. "We're sorry too."

"Now that Romeo has all our powers, it's going to take all of us working together to stop him!" Gekko announces.

Owlette teaches her friends some flying tricks. Soon Gekko and Catboy are whizzing through the air like flying experts!

"This *is* pretty cool," Owlette admits. "I didn't notice how much fun it is to share my powers with you."

The PJ Masks surround Romeo.

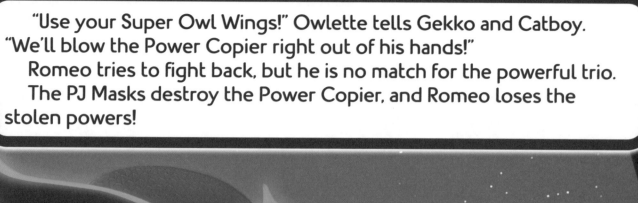

"Use your Super Owl Wings!" Owlette tells Gekko and Catboy. "We'll blow the Power Copier right out of his hands!"

Romeo tries to fight back, but he is no match for the powerful trio. The PJ Masks destroy the Power Copier, and Romeo loses the stolen powers!

The PJ Masks have saved the school, and now Owlette knows that it's more fun to share with friends!

PJ Masks all shout hooray! 'Cause in the night, we saved the day!